This book belongs to:

....

Note to parents and carers

Read it yourself is a series of classic, traditional tales, written in a simple way to give children a confident and successful start to reading.

Each book is carefully structured to include many high-frequency words that are vital for first reading. The sentences on each page are supported closely by pictures to help with reading, and to offer lively details to talk about.

The books are graded into four levels that progressively introduce wider vocabulary and longer stories as a reader's ability grows.

Ideas for use

- Begin by looking through the book and talking about the pictures. Has your child heard this story before?

- Help her with any words she does not know, either by helping her to sound them out or supplying them yourself.

- Developing readers can be concentrating so hard on the words that they sometimes don't fully grasp the meaning of what they're reading. Answering the puzzle questions on pages 30 and 31 will help with understanding.

For more information and advice, visit www.ladybird.com/readityourself

Level 2 is ideal for children who have received some reading instruction and can read short, simple sentences with help.

Special features:

Frequent repetition of main story words and phrases

Short, simple sentences

Large, clear type

Little Red Riding Hood's father was in the forest.

He ran to Grandmother's door with his big axe.

27

Little Red Riding Hood lived with her mother and father in a house in the forest.

Careful match between story and pictures

7

Educational Consultant: Geraldine Taylor

A catalogue record for this book is available from the British Library

Published by Ladybird Books Ltd
80 Strand, London, WC2R 0RL
A Penguin Company

004 - 10 9 8 7 6 5 4
© LADYBIRD BOOKS LTD MMX
Ladybird, Read It Yourself and the Ladybird Logo are registered or
unregistered trade marks of Ladybird Books Limited.

ISBN: 978-1-40930-360-2

Printed in China

Little Red Riding Hood

Illustrated by Diana Mayo

Little Red Riding Hood lived with her mother and father in a house in the forest.

One day Little Red Riding Hood's mother said, "Will you take these cakes to Grandmother?"

"Yes," said Little Red Riding Hood, and off she went.

Grandmother's house was on the other side of the forest. And in the forest lived a wolf.

When the wolf saw Little
Red Riding Hood he said,
"I will eat her all up!"
And off he ran.

Little Red Riding Hood
knocked on her
grandmother's door.

"Come in," said
a funny voice.

14

Little Red Riding Hood
looked at her grandmother.

"Come closer, my dear,"
said the funny voice.

29

How much do you remember about the story of Little Red Riding Hood? Answer these questions and find out!

- Where is Little Red Riding Hood going?

- Who sees her in the forest?

- Who is the wolf pretending to be?

- Who rescues Little Red Riding Hood and Grandmother?

Look at the pictures and match them to the story words.

wolf

father

grandmother

forest

Little Red Riding Hood

Read it yourself
with Ladybird

The Three Billy Goats Gruff

Cinderella

Little Red Hen

Goldilocks and the Three Bears

The Magic Porridge Pot

The Ugly Duckling

The Gingerbread Man

Sleeping Beauty

Sly Fox and Red Hen

The Three Little Pigs

Town Mouse and Country Mouse

Little Red Riding Hood

The Elves and the Shoemaker

Jack and the Beanstalk

The Pied Piper of Hamelin

The Wizard of Oz

Collect all the titles in the series.